THE
NGUYEN KIDS

The Power of the
PEARL EARRINGS

written by
Linda Trinh

illustrated by
Clayton Nguyen

annick
press
toronto · berkeley

Cover art by Clayton Nguyen, designed by Paul Covello
Interior designed by Paul Covello and Aldo Fierro
Edited by Katie Hearn
Copy edited by Eleanor Gasparik
Proofread by Mary Ann Blair

Annick Press Ltd.

We acknowledge the support of the Canada Council for the Arts and
the Ontario Arts Council, and the participation of the Government
of Canada/la participation du gouvernement du Canada for our
publishing activities.

Library and Archives Canada Cataloguing in Publication

Title: The power of the pearl earrings / written by Linda Trinh ; illustrated by Clayton Nguyen.
Names: Trinh, Linda, author. | Nguyen, Clayton, illustrator.
Description: "The Nguyen kids"--Cover.
Identifiers: Canadiana 20220167834 | ISBN 9781773217109 (hardcover) | ISBN 9781773217116
(softcover)
Classification: LCC PS8639.R575 P69 2022 | DDC jC813/.6—dc23

Published in the U.S.A. by Annick Press (U.S.) Ltd.
Distributed in Canada by University of Toronto Press.
Distributed in the U.S.A. by Publishers Group West.

Printed in Canada

annickpress.com
lindaytrinh.com
claytonnguyen.art

Also available as an e-book. Please visit annickpress.com/ebooks for more details.

For Ryan, our stories are forever intertwined.
—L.T.

For Maddy.
—C.N.

TABLE OF CONTENTS

CHAPTER 1

I'm the Leader!

"Now what, Liz?" Rohan, Best Friend Ever, asks me. He grabs a handful of ketchup chips.

I shrug. We're hanging out in my living room. It's the Sunday before school starts and it's raining. It's so boring being trapped inside.

"Let's play Trung Warriors!" I stand up quickly. "To practice for our first Taekwondo class."

"Okay!" Rohan says as he leaps onto the couch.

"You were Trưng Trắc last time. I'm the leader!" I move to stand in front of him. "I'm at the front of the elephant. You're my sister, Trưng Nhị."

My Grandma Nội used to babysit me and Rohan. My grandma used to tell us the story of Hai Bà Trưng, two brave sisters who lived a long time ago. They were warriors, great fighters, and fought for freedom. They were Vietnamese like I am.

"The invaders are coming!" I shout and pull out my imaginary sword.

Rohan pulls out his imaginary sword too. We jump from our elephant to fight the bad guys.

I get my short hair stuck on one of my pearl

earrings when I do a spin kick move. The pearl earrings were a gift from Grandma Nội. My sister got our grandma's jade bangle. And my brother got her painted fan. My gift is the coolest.

I look over at Grandma Nội's picture on her altar in our dining room. She died over a year ago now. Dad and Mom say we Vietnamese believe the spirits of our family, our ancestors, stay with us after they pass away. They hear our prayers. They watch out for us. I hope she's happy I'm wearing her earrings.

"The other fighters are too strong! To the river," Rohan says, just like we've played so many times. He runs to the window.

I jab and duck and fight my way over to him.

We are back-to-back as we swing our invisible swords around. I throw cushions and pillows everywhere.

Me and Rohan lie on the floor after the battle.

That's how my older sister, Miss Perfect, Anne, finds me. Dad and Mom are always busy with her and my younger brother, The Baby, Jacob. I get lost in the middle most of the time.

Dad always said it's Anne's job as the oldest sister to look after us. She's only two years older than me. I'm eight, but she thinks she's the boss of me.

"Hey, we have to practice," Anne says.

My boring sister and her boring ballet friends, Sophie and Jennifer, want to wreck my fun, again.

"We were here first. Basement?" I reply.

"The floor here is better. You go to the basement!" she says.

"Mom!" we yell at the same time.

Mom comes in from the kitchen. "Liz, Rohan, please! The girls have a performance." She gives me that look—*don't make trouble.*

"My mom always sides with Anne," I say as

Rohan and I head down the basement stairs. I stomp my feet.

"At least she let you quit ballet," Rohan replies.

It's true. Before Anne changed ballet schools, Mom would never have let me. Now she asks questions about how I'm feeling and if things bother me. But there's one thing that hasn't changed. She still sides with my sister!

Rohan punches in the air. "And now we'll both be in Mrs. Goodman's grade three class and take Taekwondo together!"

I nod, happy again. "We can be like the Trung Warriors for real!" I say, kicking into the air.

CHAPTER 2
Golden Boy

"I like your earrings," my friend Lucy says to me a few days later on the first day of school.

I smile as I sit at the desk beside her. "Thanks, I like your shoes!"

I look around. New classroom! New teacher! I can't wait! I touch my earrings and feel a rush of wind. I can almost hear Grandma Nội's laughter through them. Weird!

Rohan sits at the desk on my other side. Gershom is in front of me. And Aiden is behind me. It's so awesome to be surrounded by friends.

Our teacher, Mrs. Goodman, stands at the front. "Welcome, everyone, to grade three. Before we do attendance, in our class, we have two students new to our school. Welcome, Rosa. Rosa's family just came to Winnipeg from the Philippines."

Rosa stands up but looks down at the floor.

I like the color of her shirt. It's pink like Auntie Hai's roses.

"And welcome, Michael," Mrs. Goodman continues.

A boy at the back stands up and waves.

Michael reminds me of the Golden Boy statue that is at the very top of an important building downtown. Shiny and cool.

"Hey! We moved from Victoria. I need a parka soon, right? Like next month?" he says.

I giggle along with some other girls. Some of the boys wave to him.

They both seem cool. Can't wait for recess to make even more friends!

Miss Perfect, our cousin Hao, and Jennifer, all in grade five, come over to say hi at morning recess. I say hey quickly and pull Rohan away. I want my own friend group and not to be Anne's tag-along sister.

I check on Jacob hanging out at the grade two doors. He's one year younger than me, seven years old. I can't help looking out for him, even though he's the baby of the family and gets everything he wants. He runs in circles with his hockey friends, Nam and Kayden. He's okay so I turn back to my friends.

Rohan and I stand in the field with Aiden, Gershom, Lucas, Madiha, and Lucy. Some other friends come over. Rohan and I start punching and kicking the air.

I wave Rosa to come over. I want her to be my friend.

"That's my fave kind of pink," I say to her.

She doesn't say anything.

I point at her pink shirt and my pink bracelet and do a thumbs-up. She smiles. And I smile even more.

Michael comes over to join us. "What's up?"

He doesn't look like the new kid. He's smiling at everyone and looking relaxed. If this was my first day at a new school, I'd so want to throw up.

"Practicing our moves," I say.

"Liz has the best moves," Aiden says.

"Gershom, you pretend to fall when I come at you," I say and step toward him.

"Way to go, Liz," Lucy says.

"Cool moves," says Michael, looking only at Rohan and not at me.

"Liz and I are starting Taekwondo together," Rohan says, as he spins around and kicks.

"That's cool, Rohan." Then he turns to me and shakes his head. "But Liz, really?" He turns to the crowd. "Taekwondo—isn't that a boy thing?"

Kids stop. And then some begin to laugh.

That is so weird to say. "No! Girls can do anything!" I say but my voice shakes.

Michael doesn't back down. He says more loudly and with a steady voice, "But girls aren't into things like that."

But *I'm* into this stuff. I love the Trung Warriors and they were women and they fought for freedom.

Lucas and Aiden laugh again. Rohan looks down and doesn't say anything. Gershom and Lucy walk away.

"Boys like that stuff," Michael says like he wants to bug me or something.

I drop my hands and my cheeks feel flushed. I don't say anything. Am I the strange one? For once, I'm not so excited to be the center of attention.

CHAPTER 3
Grandma Nội's Gifts

Rohan and I wait for our first Taekwondo class to start. We sit cross-legged in our white uniforms. We thumb wrestle as we wait. I win most of the games, as usual. We laugh but try not to be too loud.

Rohan says, "Want to go to the new superhero movie this weekend?"

I shake my head. "Can't. Mid-Autumn Festival. What about next weekend?"

Like me, he also celebrates holidays that a lot of other kids, the white kids, don't. We get each other.

We've been best friends since kindergarten when we both came to school dressed as superheroes for Halloween. We ran around in our capes all day. Since then, we've pretended to be lots of heroes and fighters and warriors together.

He nods. "Sure. Maybe we can ask Michael?"

"Why? He was so rude to me," I reply. I still feel so embarrassed thinking about how the kids laughed at me.

"He's by himself. He likes role-playing too and

video games. He's cool, but he wants to play with me," Rohan says.

I feel a rush of wind and I touch my earrings. That's weird. Before I can tell Rohan he's cool too, our instructor comes in.

"Hello. I'm Master Kim. Stand up. Let's bow and begin," he says.

That evening, I'm helping Miss Perfect put the đồ chua pickled carrots and daikon in glass jars. After feeling confused from Taekwondo, I'm happy she asked me.

Anne's jade bangle gently taps against the jar.

That was Grandma's gift to her. I touch my earrings.

"Do you ever feel something weird with the bangle?" I ask.

"Like what?" she says.

"Like it's windy even when you're inside?" I'm not even sure what I'm saying.

She nods. "That's Grandma Nội. To let you know she's with you."

"Oh!" I pause with my chopsticks in the air. "What does she want?"

My sister smiles at me and I can't help but smile back.

Anne says, "Let's just say I thought I was helping her but, really, she helped me. If you need help, she'll know."

"How?" I ask.

She holds up her bangle. She points at my earrings. "Grandma Nội's gifts. The pearl earrings connect you to her. It's the secret between you. She would tell me stories of the family. Like she knew I needed to hear them."

I nod. "She used to tell me the story about Hai Bà Trưng. I sooo needed to hear their story."

Sometimes I got angry at myself for not being as good as Miss Perfect. Or sad that The Baby got

all the attention. Grandma Nội would tell me I'm like Trưng Trắc, I'm important. And I'm like Trưng Nhị, I'm loved. I've always loved their story because my grandma loved their story.

Anne holds my hand. "Like I said, if you need help, Grandma Nội will know."

I touch my earrings again. Nhị had her older sister Trắc to look out for her. Anne does that for me. But I would never admit that to her!

CHAPTER 4
Quick to Act

Monday doesn't come fast enough! I can't wait to see my friends! During our rocks and minerals unit in class, Mrs. Goodman asks, "What are the three kinds of rock?"

Both me and Michael raise our hands.

"Michael!" She points to him.

"Igneous, sedimentary, and metamorphic," he

says in a loud voice.

"Very good, Michael!" Mrs. Goodman says.

Grrr. The teacher keeps calling on him before me.

Michael is, as my sister would say, super smart. Mrs. Goodman, the music teacher, the gym teacher—they all love him. Shiny and cool like the Golden Boy downtown.

Mrs. Goodman asks another question. Golden Boy Michael has his hand up again, so why bother trying?

To get a break from him, I'm excited when it's time for recess. Outside, me and Madiha are doing cartwheels in the field.

"You're so good at that, Liz," Rosa says. She

and Lucy join in.

"Thanks," I reply. I see some boys going to play basketball. That looks fun! I do a few more cartwheels then run over.

"Hey, pass the ball," I say to Lucas.

"Sorry, Lizzie, we already have enough players," Michael says.

"My name is Liz," I say.

Michael begins to walk toward the court. Rohan starts to walk after him.

"Hey, Rohan, when I come over later, I'll bring some Vietnamese jelly my sister made," I say.

Michael turns back around. "Rohan is coming over to my house tonight."

Rohan looks down at the ground. "Sorry, Liz.

He invited me, and we hang out all the time, so I thought . . ."

"What?" I whisper.

Rohan always has time for me, unlike my parents. He was an only child most of the time we've been friends until his baby sister Rakina was born last year. It's always me and him. Even with other friends around, I know we're best friends.

"Later, Lizzie," Golden Boy says as they both walk away.

I feel like I'm going to throw up.

"Not hanging out at Rohan's today?" Dad asks that night at Jacob's hockey practice.

I'm doing my Vietnamese homework. Dad, me, and Anne work with a tutor. It's sooo hard I get mad at myself. Con cá, trái cà, con gà. Fish, tomato, chicken. What's with all the tones? Why am I even learning this? This won't help me with my friends. So boring!

I shake my head. "He's at the new kid's house. Michael."

"Yes, that's it," Dad murmurs to himself as he looks over at Jacob on the ice, and then turns to me. "Huh?"

The Baby and Dad are buddies. Miss Perfect and Mom are buddies. Mom and Dad just want me to stay out of the way. That's why I'm usually with Rohan.

I shrug. "It's like Michael only wants to play with boys. Like he thinks boys are cooler," I say.

Jacob comes over for some water, his cheeks looking sweaty.

"Keep working on your crossovers, okay, buddy?" Dad says.

"Okay," Jacob replies and skates off again.

"That's it, that's good, Jacob!" Dad shouts.

I try again, louder this time, to get his attention. "Michael doesn't like me."

"It's hard to be new. Like my clients coming from other countries. Try to make friends with him," Dad says, his eyes still on Jacob, as usual.

Rohan wants to be friends with him. So maybe that's not a bad idea.

Mom named all of us after characters from her favorite storybooks. Jacob is from *Jacob Two-Two Meets the Hooded Fang*. Anne is from *Anne of Green Gables*. And I'm Elizabeth from *The Paper Bag Princess*. And just like the paper bag princess, I need to make a good plan.

I need a plan to make Michael my friend. To make Michael like me. Then Rohan will play with me again. Why didn't I think of this earlier?

Grandma Nội used to say I'm so quick—quick to decide, quick to change my mind, and quick to act. She was right. I want to do this right now!

I feel a rush of wind and I touch my pearl earrings. I wonder. Grandma Nội, is that you? This Make-Golden-Boy-My-Friend Plan is going to be sooo awesome!

CHAPTER 5
Mid-Autumn Festival

"I'm ready," I call out to the family as I race to the car. Yay, it's Tết Trung Thu, Mid-Autumn Festival! When we get to Favorite Auntie Hai and Uncle Hai's house, Anne and I go over to Grandma Nội's altar to say hi by bowing our heads. It's like the altar we have at home.

After dinner, Cool Cousin Hanh and me and

my brother are in the living room. Hanh is in high school and has her own phone. She's teaching me and Jacob the fan dance that she's learning at the Vietnamese Buddhist temple. Anne and Hao are doing dishes. Mom and Auntie are getting dessert together. I don't know where the dads went.

"Again!" Jacob says, waving the two fans around him. One of the fans is Grandma Nội's painted fan he got last year, with the twelve animals of the Vietnamese zodiac on it. The dog chases the rooster who runs after the monkey.

Hanh goes through the moves again and we all spin and jump, turning our fans.

Grandpa Nội watches us from his comfy chair and claps when we're done.

"Đẹp quá." He says that it's so beautiful.

I hug Jacob and tickle him. He runs over to Grandpa for help but Grandpa tickles him too.

I close my fans and pretend they are sticks and start punching with them instead.

"Liz, like Taekwondo?" Grandpa asks.

"It's great, Grandpa! It's fun."

But then I remember what Michael said and how all the kids laughed. When I think of Taekwondo now, there is a cloud of weirdness over it.

"Mooncakes!" Mom says. She puts a platter on the low table in front of Grandpa Nội.

I touch the pearl earring on my right ear. "What about Grandma Nội?" I ask.

"I already put a cake on her altar," Anne replies.

Favorite Auntie says, "In Vietnam, Tết Trung Thu for family get together. After good harvest, we say thank you. We eat bánh trung thu."

Mom points to the different cakes. "That is double yolk. This one is only lotus paste. This one has nuts."

I take a slice of the double-yolk cake and give it to Grandpa Nội. I take a slice with nuts and hand it to Hao behind me.

"Thanks, Liz, you know my fave," Hao says.

I grab one with no yolk for myself. It's sweet inside with an outer shell like a pie crust.

Anne says between bites, "Maybe I can try making mooncakes next year."

Everyone nods.

"Lantern time," Grandpa Nội says and hands out paper lanterns. There are different shapes and animals, and they have fake lights inside. "Walk. Go."

Hanh sits out and so does Anne, thinking she's too old now. Hao gets a lantern with me and Jacob.

Like we do every year, we walk around the house and through the garage and back inside with our lanterns. Dad and Uncle Hai, hiding in the garage, nod and clap.

My pearl earrings feel nice against my ears. I feel strong. The wind rushes around me, like I'm caught up in a hug.

I whisper to the air, "Grandma Nội, I love you."

Here with my family, I know girls can do anything. I can do anything.

CHAPTER 6
The Trung Aunties

"Twenty high punches. Twenty middle punches. Twenty low punches. Go," Master Kim shouts from the front of the class.

"Yes, sir," I say and start my punches.

I look over at Rohan in the next row. I wave. He waves quickly then looks away.

"Now, some kicks," Master Kim continues.

"Kicking stance. Rising kick. Begin. Hana."

I start to kick as Master Kim counts in Korean. Straight leg as high as I can go.

"Dool."

Kick. Why is Rohan ignoring me?

"Set."

Kick. Why doesn't Michael like me?

"Net."

Kick. When will my Make-Golden-Boy-My-Friend Plan work?

"Dah-sut."

Kick.

   Kick.

      Kick.

There are so many feelings inside me.

I hear a sound like wind whistling through trees.

What is that?

Energy flows through me.

What is that?

I stop kicking. I touch the pearls and I can sense energy through my body.

"Liz, it's not break time yet," Master Kim points out. Then he says to the whole class, "Front snap kick. Begin. Hana."

I raise my leg and snap my lower leg out, from the knee.

You are like Trưng Trắc.

You are important.

What?

43

You are like Trưng Nhị.

You are loved.

Is that the Trung Warriors? How can I hear them?

My fists are closed tight at my sides.

Grandma Nội used to say those words to me when she knew I needed to hear them. Is Anne right about Grandma helping me?

I look around. No one else seems to sense them.

I try kicking again. The energy is still there and I can still feel the wind.

And is Anne right about it coming through my earrings?

"Good work, Liz. Good power," Master Kim says.

I smile widely.

On Sunday, Grandpa Nội is home with Hao and Jacob. Uncle Hai and Dad are working. Mom takes Hanh and Anne shopping, but I think shopping is boring. I hang out with Favorite Auntie at the nail salon.

I set up all the nail polish bottles in the glass cabinet, still thinking about the Trung Warriors and Taekwondo. A man walks in.

"Can help you?" Auntie Hai asks him.

"Yes. I. Need. A. Gift. Certificate. One. Hundred. Dollars," he shouts slowly.

After he leaves, I turn to my aunt. "Why did he talk like that?"

She laughs. "Man looks at me. Speaks slow. Like I am stupid, my English not perfect. I write poetry in Vietnamese. I know things." She sits up taller and lifts her chin.

I nod. Favorite Auntie does know a lot of things.

"Auntie, I think Trưng Trắc and Trưng Nhị are visiting me. Is that sooo crazy?" I ask.

She doesn't laugh or make me feel dumb. Instead, she tilts her head and thinks about it. That's why she's my favorite. "In Vietnam, Hai

Bà Trưng prayed to. We believe their spirits still around."

I nod. "Like Grandma Nội is still with us."

"Do they visit you?" Auntie Hai shrugs. "Only you know. They know you need help. They come. Like your aunties. You listen to them."

I touch my earrings. I think Grandma Nội knows I need

their bravery and energy. She must have sent them to help me. The Trung Aunties are here to help me with my Make-Golden-Boy-My-Friend Plan! I know it!

CHAPTER 7
"No Girls Allowed" Club

"You're It for tag!" I call to Rohan during morning recess a few days later.

"Not now, Liz," he says. He's with Michael and other boys collecting sticks near the back fence.

I close my eyes. My cheeks are hot.

Rosa and Lucy are on the play structure, and they wave me over. But I don't feel like playing with them today. All they do is sit around and talk. Instead, I slowly walk over to Anne, her friend Jennifer, and Hao jumping around puddles.

But I only want to play with Rohan. We like the same things. Who will role-play with me now? Who will just let me be myself?

I jump around with Anne, but I keep looking at Rohan having fun without me. There's an emptiness in my chest. It hurts that he doesn't have time for me. Can I even still call him Best Friend Ever?

I get to talk to Rohan as he puts on his jacket for lunchtime recess. The boys left without him.

"Rohan, hey," I say.

He looks around, maybe to make sure we are

alone. It makes my chest hurt even more.

"Hey," he whispers.

"How was Rakina's first birthday?" I ask.

He's about to talk about his sister when Golden Boy comes back in.

"Lizzie, did Rohan tell you what we did on the weekend? I started the 'No Girls Allowed' Club. I'm president. Rohan is vice-president," he says.

I look at Rohan but he looks down.

"Can I join too?" I ask, not knowing what else to say.

"You're a girl, aren't you, Lizzie?" Michael asks.

"So? I can do anything you do," I say. "Please?" My voice is quiet.

Michael walks away first. "Sorry, boys only. How about you paint your nails or go shopping. Let's go, Rohan."

"Really?" I ask Rohan.

"Come on, Liz. We can't play Trung Warriors forever! Michael and Lucas are cool. The boys," he says.

"The white boys?" I ask.

He shrugs and runs off.

Michael has so many friends. Why does he want my best friend too?

I want to cry. I run my hands down the side of my body, forcing all those feelings down. I won't let the boys see me cry.

I feel the wind on my face.

You are like Trưng Trắc.

You are important.

You are like Trưng Nhị.

You are loved.

No. No. No.

I take off the pearl earrings and shove them

into the bottom of my backpack. Rohan picked Michael over me. So how can I be important or loved? The Trung Aunties are no help. Time to move on and try something else.

What is it about me that Michael doesn't like? Because I'm a girl? Well, I'll show him.

CHAPTER 8

One of the Boys

"Okay, class, for our next science unit, we'll be learning how to code," Mrs. Goodman says the next day at school.

I'm so distracted thinking about Michael and Rohan I almost miss it.

"That means giving directions to a computer to do things. You'll work in pairs and share the laptops," she continues.

This is going to be so awesome! Right away, I look over at Rohan, forgetting for a second that he's my Ex–Best Friend Ever now. Rohan doesn't see me. He turns around to Michael. A lot of the boys in class do that too.

"I have everyone's name in this box," says Mrs. Goodman and pulls out a name. "Hayden and"— she pulls out another name—"Rohan." She pulls out more names, "Rosa and Madiha. Lucy and Lucas. Liz and Michael."

Us together? That's sooo great! I can get him to like me. Then he'll let me join his club. Then Rohan will be Best Friend Ever again. I sit up straighter. I wave at him, and he shrugs.

We sit next to each other at a laptop. I look at the handout. "So we have to look at ways to make the letters of our name move and change," I say.

"Cool." Golden Boy pulls the laptop toward him and clicks around the screen. Nothing happens. "Here, you try," he says finally.

I look at the instructions. "Okay, pick the letter objects." I find the letters for *L-I-Z*.

"Cool. My turn." He pushes forward again.

"I wasn't done yet," I say.

He gets the letters for his first name. "Now, I do this and this." He drags a few code blocks to the coding area. Nothing happens when he presses the start button.

"I don't think that's right." I look at the instructions again.

"Sure it is. You change the looks for each object and then loop it and you can clone it."

He seems so sure of himself, but what he says doesn't make any sense. Is he just pretending?

"Then you do it," he says finally.

I work on his letters. When I'm done, one letter spins, one grows and shrinks, and others change color or do another cool animation. "There!"

"Nice! You're okay, Lizzie," he replies.

I touch my ears, forgetting that I took off Grandma Nội's pearl earrings. This proves I don't need the Trung Aunties to impress Michael.

I smile widely. I can be one of the boys.

After dinner, it's so different that just me and Mom are home.

Mom is looking at her phone. I sit right next to her with the laptop.

"Mom, do you want to see what I'm doing?" I ask.

"One second, honey," she replies. "Next weekend, you kids are going to help Auntie Hai with some basement cleanup, okay?" She texts and I wait.

I nod. "Okay. Look, I'm coding for class," I say.

Mom looks at my screen. "That's a fun program. Nice colored blocks. Better than the ones the guys and I use at work," she says.

I know Mom works with computers at an office downtown, near the Golden Boy building. Maybe she knows things too, like Favorite Auntie does. "Mom, do you work with a lot of guys? Do you feel weird sometimes?"

"How?" she asks.

I shrug. "Like they tell you things you already know. Or they pretend to know things. Like people pay more attention to them."

"All the time!" She texts again. "And men I've trained get better jobs before I do. It's extra hard because I'm female and Asian." Mom looks up from her phone. "Are guys, are boys, doing this at school?"

Last year, Anne faced racism at her old ballet school. My sister was so sad, then Mom and Dad got mad. Racism is when people are treated unfairly because of the color of their skin. Mom is trying to ask more questions now. Both Mom and

Dad talk now about things that I don't understand or that I need them to explain.

I want to tell her about Michael, but I don't want to be trouble. She says she and Dad are busy providing for us.

I shake my head.

Mom puts her phone away. "Liz, you can tell me anything. I know Grandma Nội used to tell you the story of Hai Bà Trưng. You're strong like they are. Don't let the boys take over."

"I'm fine." I will prove to Michael I'm good enough to join his club. I will get Rohan back. Then everything will be so great again.

CHAPTER 9
What's Wrong with Me?

I get the chance to make everything so great again when it's time to present our coding projects in class. Since I have lots of time to work on my coding at home. Since Rohan stopped asking me to come over.

"Michael and Liz, your turn." Mrs. Goodman calls us to show the class our animated names.

I don't wear Grandma Nội's pearl earrings

anymore. I don't need the energy or the help of the Trung Aunties. My Make-Golden-Boy-My-Friend Plan will soon work. He'll have to like me after being coding partners.

I pull up what we've done on the projected screen. The word "Michael" shows up.

Before I can talk, Michael steps in front of me. He says, "I tried a bunch of things with the letters," and he presses play. All his letters do something really cool.

Everyone claps.

"Way to go, Michael!" Aiden says.

"Yay, Mikey!" Lucas shouts.

"Great job, that's a lot more than we have seen," Mrs. Goodman says.

"Liz helped," Michael says.

Mrs. Goodman looks at me. "It's nice Michael was able to help you. Glad you two work well together." She turns back to the class. "Rosa and Madiha now."

What is happening?

Michael didn't help me! I coded the whole thing. He just pressed one button. My ears burn red hot. I can't believe it.

At recess, I run over to where the "No Girls Allowed" Club meets near the back fence.

Michael sees me coming and walks toward me, away from the other boys.

"I did the work. The class and the teacher think you did it all," I say.

"Not my problem," he replies.

"What?" I ask.

"Everyone expects me to be good at everything. To be better than everyone. You try being the new kid!" He walks away.

I feel like there's a big hole inside me. Michael doesn't care about me. He only cares about himself! If only he knew how bad this felt. I start to feel hot around my neck. I'll show him!

I look around. I see Anne and she's with Jacob. She's putting his toque back on and zipping up his jacket.

My knees are wobbly as I run over to them.

I hug my sister and bury my face in her shoulder.

"Liz?" she asks.

"Why doesn't he like me? What's wrong with me?" I begin to cry. "And my teacher thinks I don't know anything." I say everything I have been holding in.

"Elizabeth, that sucks." Anne wraps her arms around me.

"And Rohan, he's not my best friend anymore," I sob.

"Then Rohan's missing out. And we're sisters." Anne holds my face between her hands like Grandma Nội used to do. I feel the jade bangle along my chin. "That means we'll be friends forever."

The bangle reminds me of my pearl earrings and the Trung Aunties. They had each other. Anne and I have each other.

Jacob hugs me from the other side. "And me. I'm here forever too," Jacob says.

I'm too quick, moving from one thing to another, Grandma Nội used to say. I was so quick I didn't see I've always had the Friends Forever Plan.

I laugh through my tears.

CHAPTER 10

All the Ancestors Are in Me

"These were all Grandma Nội's?" I point at a box full of áo dài fabric, all different colors, some silky, some glittery, all awesome!

Me, Anne, and Jacob are over at Favorite Auntie's house. Mom volunteered us to help clean out some of Grandma's stuff from the basement. It's so much work, but it's also fun seeing all her old things.

"She collect them. Love them," Favorite Auntie replies.

We work for sooo long sorting stuff. Anne, Hanh, and Hao all go up for a TV break.

"Auntie Hai, can I have this?" Jacob wraps himself in soft purple áo dài fabric with the image of a phoenix embroidered on it. As he spins around, glitter flies everywhere.

Of course, she'll say yes. He gets everything he wants.

"Lấy đi con." Our aunt tells him to take it.

"Cám ơn." Jacob says thank you and runs up the stairs.

I start to follow him.

"Liz, come here," says Favorite Auntie, waving

me over.

I sit on the floor with her.

"Why you not wear earrings? Bà Nội's earrings?" Favorite Auntie asks as she holds up some sparkly yellow fabric and hands it to me.

I touch my ears and shrug. I begin to fold the fabric back up and put it in the "keep" box.

"Do Hai Bà Trưng still visit you?" She holds up pink fabric and puts it into the "give away" plastic bag. "You listen?"

I shake my head.

"Why not?" She stops working and looks right at me.

I pick at my fingernails. "Boys do what they want. People pay more attention to them, listen to to them, think they're smarter. How can Hai Bà Trưng help me?" I feel an emptiness inside me.

Favorite Auntie shakes her head. "They fight for freedom. For others. They do what no men do." She puts her hand on mine. "Be proud to be a girl."

I'm silent.

Favorite Auntie keeps talking. "You from Hai Bà Trưng. Vietnam's first feminists."

"What are feminists?" I ask and pay closer attention.

"Us feminists believe women equal to men. Should have same rights and chances. Still need to fight," she says.

"Then I'm a feminist too!" I shout out.

Favorite Auntie says, "Your great-grandmother.

Grandmother. Mother. Me. All strong. You from a line of strong women."

You are like Trưng Trắc.

You are important.

You are like Trưng Nhị.

You are loved.

"Do you know what Grandma Nội told me?" Anne says from the stairs where she has been listening. She's been watching me closely since I cried at recess. She wears glasses now and loves pushing them up her nose like she does now.

I shrug.

Anne comes over and puts her hand on my chest. "All the ancestors are in you."

"All the ancestors are in me," I repeat. My

ancestors were strong.

"You are Liz Nguyen. Be proud of yourself," Anne says.

"Do what only you can do," Favorite Auntie adds.

I smile and pull both Anne and Favorite Auntie into a hug-me sandwich.

At home that night, before bed, I decide to put the earrings back on, wanting to feel the connection to Grandma Nội and to the Trung Aunties. To figure out what to do next, I could use help. I feel like Elizabeth from *The Paper Bag Princess*. And like her, I'll be happy in the end. But what will make me happy? I know right away. Michael: unhappy. Michael: being embarrassed and sad, like I was. Let's see how Michael likes it! I have the Best-Get-Back-at-Golden-Boy Plan now.

I don't know if the Trung Aunties will like this, but I push that thought aside. I can't wait to start my new plan!

CHAPTER 11

What's Really Going On

There are only a few boys hanging out in the "No Girls Allowed" Club at morning recess on Monday.

"What happened with them?" I ask Lucy as I sit with her and Rosa at the play structure.

"A bunch were over at Michael's house yesterday. Aiden and him got into a fight. And

Lucas called him a know-it-all," Lucy answers, since she is Lucas's coding partner.

"Good! Doesn't let girls play. Stupid," Rosa adds.

"I agree, Rosa!" I say and we all laugh.

After recess, we look at animation more closely for the coding unit. I'm looking at Michael, and he doesn't seem so golden now. I know now he's pretending to know things. He's more like pyrite we learned about in the rocks and minerals unit. Fake gold.

"Mrs. Goodman," Lucas says. "I want the letter *L* to grow and shrink but nothing happens after I press start."

"Okay, let's look at this as a class." She

pulls up the coding program on the projected screen.

I see my chance! The Best-Get-Back-at-Golden-Boy Plan! My hand shoots up in the air. "Mrs. Goodman, Michael and I can show the class."

Mrs. Goodman nods. "Wonderful idea!"

"Michael, you do it. Write the code. Just like for our project," I say to him in the next row.

His eyes widen. I think he starts to shake his head.

"Go, Michael!" Gershom says.

"Yeah, Michael!" Hayden adds.

He has to look good in front of the boys.

"Go ahead, Michael," says the teacher.

He gets up to the front of the class. And he starts to click around the screen.

"Ummm," he says—he pulls up the *M* letter object—"here."

He slowly clicks through the different code blocks.

Kids start to look at each other.

Michael's cheeks are red. He starts to pace.

Kids start to giggle.

"Come on, Michael!" Hayden whispers.

Mrs. Goodman asks, "Is everything okay?"

Michael looks at the door.

Now he's going to know how bad it was for me. Not so golden anymore. He's going to be sooo embarrassed.

I try to sink into how good this feels. My plan is working.

But the good feeling I expected isn't there.

Seeing Michael up there, I don't feel important, like I thought I would.

I actually feel bad for him. So bad.

There's no energy from the Trung Aunties. I'm not

proud of myself now, and I know Grandma Nội wouldn't be.

I need to fix what I've done. Anne said the ancestors are in me. They were strong and brave, so I know what I need to do to fix this. I raise my hand. "I'll do it. Michael presented last time." I go to the front.

Michael hurries back to his seat.

I add the letters of my name. I pull code blocks. "Use the 'start' control block and add the 'forever' code block. Use the 'change the size by twenty-five' to grow. Use the 'change the size by minus twenty-five' to shrink. But the computer moves really quickly."

I go to the "wait one second" code block and

add one block before each "change" block, while explaining, "You need to pause, slow things down. Then you can see what's really going on." I click "start" and the *L* grows and shrinks and grows and shrinks.

A wonderful energy fills me, warm and sparkling.

You are like Trưng Trắc.

You are important.

You are like Trưng Nhị.

You are loved.

Like with the computer, I also need to pause. I can't always be so quick, like Grandma Nội used to say. Now I see I already have what I wanted. I am important. I am loved.

"That's what I was missing," Lucas says.

"I see that," Lucy exclaims.

A few kids nod their heads.

"Way to go, Liz!" Rohan says.

Mrs. Goodman says, "Great work, Liz!"

This time it's my name on the projected screen,

L-I-Z.

CHAPTER 12
You Okay?

During Friday's lunchtime recess that week, Lucy, Lucas, Hayden, and Rosa all want to play tag.

Anne starts to walk over to me, but I give her a thumbs-up. She goes back to Jennifer and Hao.

Rohan joins me and says, "Come on, Liz, you can be It."

I see Michael sitting by himself again on a bench. He hasn't hung out with anyone all week.

I still have the warm energy around me. It's the energy of the Trung Aunties even though I don't need their help the way I did before. "I'll be there soon," I reply to Rohan.

I walk over to Michael. He is playing with his scarf.

"You okay?" I ask him.

"You must be happy. You won!" he shoots back.

"Why is it win or lose?" I ask.

He looks up. "The first day of school. You had everything. Everyone wants to be around you."

I don't say anything.

He shrugs. "Our family moves around a

lot. I'm always the new kid. I just want to have friends."

My mom said not to let the boys take over, so I reply, "Being mean, and putting down girls, and taking over—that's not cool!"

He shrugs again. "Shouldn't I be the coolest? Have everything? People always tell me I'm strong and smart."

I think of superhero movies. "If you have all that, use your powers for good then."

He nods.

"And?" I ask.

"Okay, I'm sorry. For being mean. For everything," he says.

"And what's my name?" I ask.

"Liz," he whispers.

"I'll start a friends club then. Everyone can join, even you." I laugh.

Michael smiles.

At Taekwondo class after school, I'm stretching at the beginning of class.

Rohan comes over and sits beside me. "Hey."

I just glare at him. Is he my Ex–Best Friend Ever or Good Friend now?

"Okay, sorry," he says.

I pretend I don't hear him and keep stretching. I feel the energy from the Trung Aunties.

"I've been a bad friend," he says.

"Yes," I say.

"What can I do?" he asks.

I can't stand not being friends with him. "I'll think of a lot of things. First, you will make it up to me by being the elephant when we play Trung Warriors. Jacob can be Trưng Nhị."

"Deal." He laughs.

"What did you guys do in the 'No Girls Allowed' Club anyways?" I ask.

He shrugs. "Nothing really. Video games in Michael's basement."

"You guys were acting dumb," I say.

"I know," he says.

"Time for push-ups. Get ready," Master Kim says.

"Yes, sir!" we both say.

"Let's see what you got," I say to Rohan as we get on our hands and feet.

"Give me your best twenty push-ups." Master Kim walks around all the kids.

Rohan looks over at me. "You're pretty good . . . for a girl!" he says, a little out of breath, his arms wobbling. "I'm kidding! I'm sorry!"

"You better be kidding!" I say and keep going, my arms feeling strong and holding me up.

I can do anything.

CHAPTER 13
So Special!

The day before my yellow stripe testing in Taekwondo, my hands shake as I get ready to talk to Mom and Dad. Anne is helping Jacob with his reading. Dad is washing dishes and Mom is putting leftovers in containers. I almost turn around. They are busy.

"Liz?" Dad asks as he rinses dishes.

"It's nothing," I say. They are busy providing for us, as Mom always says.

Mom puts the containers in the fridge. "You can tell us."

She gives my dad a *pay attention* look and he turns to face me.

I don't want to be trouble. But the Trung Aunties have helped me to know I am important. I take a deep breath and look at my slippers. "So tomorrow is my testing. Do you think you can come? Both of you? For the whole thing? It's okay if you can't," I say quickly, closing my eyes.

Dad kneels down in front of me. "Of course we're coming. The whole family!"

"Really?" I ask.

"We're all excited. Our own warrior!" Mom says.

Dad looks at me. "When you wear Bà Nội's earrings, I see her in you. You're both so strong," Dad says and hugs me.

I smile so widely, feeling wonderful energy flow through me.

I wake up the next day with the same energy humming inside me. Rohan and I try hard to stand still in line as we wait our turns.

I wave at my family in the front row—Mom, Dad, Miss Perfect, The Baby, Favorite Auntie,

Uncle Hai, Cool Cousin, Hao, and Grandpa Nội. I know that Grandma Nội is here too. Jacob holds up the sign he drew that says: "Go Liz Go!" There's a stick figure with a belt tied around the waist. The stick figure is kicking in the air.

I feel so special that they are all here for me!

I tie back my short hair so it doesn't get caught in my pearl earrings.

I make a funny face at Rohan a couple rows over, and he laughs.

Testing begins and I get into my horse-riding stance to show different punches and blocks. Then I do kicks. Kicks are my total fave!

"Congratulations, Liz," Master Kim says and ties on my new yellow stripe belt.

I bow. "Thank you."

After the testing, everyone comes over to our house for pizza and cake. Anne has made chả giò spring rolls. Everyone loves them! Rohan's mom brings over pani walalu honey rings for dessert.

Our friends are all busy eating and playing together. Anne and Jacob and I are lying on the floor in the living room, our heads all close together. I've eaten so much and can't move.

"Your hair is getting so long, Jacob. Will Mom cut it soon?" Anne asks.

"No. I like it long," he says.

"I do too," I say. "Can we play Trung Warriors all together after the party?"

"No, let's draw together or do the fan dance," Jacob says, sitting up.

Anne nods. "We can do both. But only after you both help me wash herbs and lettuce. I want to make bánh xèo."

I sigh and sit up too.

"No one likes that job," Jacob and I say together. We hear Mom and Dad say that all the time.

We all laugh.

"It's Grandma Nội's recipe for the fold-over pancakes. We can feel closer to her," Anne says.

"Okay," I say.

I look over at Grandma Nội's picture on the altar in the dining room. I touch my pearl earrings, her gift to me. The energy of my ancestors flows through me. I know my ancestors are strong women. I know I am important and loved.

All About Liz and Her Family

Liz Nguyen is eight years old and she's in grade three. She can't wait to start breaking boards in her Taekwondo class to show everyone how strong she is. She thinks the coolest thing about autumn is jumping into huge piles of leaves with her friends.

Jacob Nguyen is seven years old and he's in grade two. He dances around the house moving like a happy snake. When autumn comes, he loves to watch Canada geese flying in the sky in the shape of a *V*.

Anne Nguyen is ten years old and she's in grade five. She's excited about her new glasses with the tie-dye frames that make her look super smart. Her favorite thing about autumn is going back to school for a fresh start and a daily routine.

Mom works with computers in a tall building downtown. Her happy place is at the gym, especially the hot yoga studio. Her idea of a fun vacation is being near water and not having to cook all the time.

Dad is a lawyer who helps people from all over the world come to Canada. His favorite foods are any kind of noodles and sauce, yum! He's never had a dog before and has always wanted a black Lab.

Cousin Hanh is sixteen years old and she's in grade eleven. She's part of many clubs at school, like ones that get donations for local food banks and shelters. For her, autumn is all about peppermint tea and the haunted corn maze.

Cousin Hao is ten years old and he's in grade five. He likes making stop-motion animation short movies with his minifigures. He can't wait for autumn to come so he can carve pumpkins into jack-o'-lanterns and pull out the gooey guts.

Grandma Nội is the best cook and she would sometimes eat dessert first before eating dinner. She collected figurines of the Vietnamese zodiac and áo dài fabric. She used to tell a lot of stories about the family and Vietnamese fairy tales.

Grandpa Nội likes to grow flowers, fruits, and vegetables. He misses the feeling of open, blue sky like when he lived on a farm in Vietnam. He can't wait for hockey playoffs every year.

Auntie Hai works at a nail salon painting people's nails. Her favorite color is red: a lucky color. She writes poetry in Vietnamese about love and family.

Uncle Hai's job is helping care for people at the hospital. His goal is to take his family back to Vietnam on vacation every three years. He likes taking pictures around the neighborhood and at the Buddhist temple.

Author's Note

Thanks so much for spending time with Liz and her family. For her story, I thought about what it means to believe in yourself, what to do when unexpected things happen, and being brave when you feel scared. This is my offering.

Having altars to the ancestors is a Vietnamese custom I grew up with after my dad passed away when I was seven years old. We made offerings of food and recognized death anniversaries. You may have your own special ways to remember loved ones.

In history books, Hai Bà Trưng, the Trung Sisters, ruled in northern Vietnam in 40 CE after fighting off invaders. But in 43 CE, they were defeated in battle. It's not clear if the sisters really did ride elephants or perished in a river. I do know they are well-known to Vietnamese people for their courage and bravery, and people pray to them. They are examples of strong Vietnamese women, and that is the idea I focused on.

A note about the language in this series: sometimes the Vietnamese words are spelled in Vietnamese with accents, and they are pronounced in Vietnamese. And sometimes the Vietnamese words have no accents and are pronounced in a way that fits with how words are pronounced in English. I've made these choices based on how I imagine the character would say them/think of them.

For example, Nguyen as a last name is written as Nguyễn in Vietnamese. I have chosen to write it as Nguyen without the accents as I imagine the siblings would write it like that at school and pronounce their last name in an English way. Yet for the names for Trưng Trắc and Trưng Nhị, I've added accents as I imagine them saying the words in Vietnamese.

Also, sometimes I have chosen to merge English and Vietnamese words. In Vietnamese, a person would call their dad's mom Bà Nội and their dad's dad Ông Nội. I have merged Grandma and Grandpa with Nội. A person would call their dad's oldest sister Cô Hai and call their dad's oldest sister's husband Dượng Hai. I merged Auntie and Uncle with Hai. I imagine this is a decision Liz's family made. It may be different with each family.

I'm so honored you chose this book. Feel free to reach out to me at lindaytrinh.com. Take care!

Linda

Acknowledgments

Much gratitude to the entire team at Annick Press for believing in and supporting The Nguyen Kids series and *The Power of the Pearl Earrings*. Thanks to Katie for being such a careful and responsive editor; it means so much to me that we could talk through anything. Thanks to Kaela, Jieun, Eleanor, and Mary Ann for their insights. Thanks to Clayton for his amazing illustrations.

Love to all my extended family and friends for their support, and thanks to those who read various drafts. Deepest appreciation to my writerly friends—encouraging words from May, Jenny, Lindsay, Tamara, Jodi, and others provided nourishment as I wrote this book. Thanks to my best friend, Mirna, for our long conversations about young readers and for always being there for me. Thanks to my cousins Ky and Bao for their perspectives and encouragement. Thanks to my big sister, Jen, for being my biggest fangirl, loving all my words, and helping me explore our Vietnamese heritage. Thanks to my husband, Ryan, for giving me the space and support to take the chance on myself to be an author.

Thanks to my kids, Lexi and Evan, who inspire me with their curiosity, bravery, kindness, and perseverance. Lexi was my first reader and offered great insights and Evan had great ideas for me. I'm so humbled that they're able to see kids like themselves in this series. Mama loves you! And of course, thanks to my mom for making this life possible for me, and for showing me every day what hard work looked like when I was growing up.

I'll be forever grateful to my dad, my grandparents, and to all my ancestors, for everything they have sacrificed and accomplished so that I may pursue my dreams!

Keep Reading for a
Sneak Peek of Book 3

The Mystery of the
PAINTED FAN

THE NGUYEN KIDS

The Mystery of the
PAINTED FAN

written by
Linda Trinh

illustrated by
Clayton Nguyen

CHAPTER 1
Go Kings Go!

BUZZZZZZZZZZ

Yes! It's my shift!

The feeling of my blades on the ice is the best as I skate toward the centre line. My teammate Kayden beats me there, so he takes the face-off to start the third period. I line up on his left like a tiger, ready to pounce. Go Kings Go!

Puck drop!

The Eagles player shoots the puck over our blue line. My teammate Emma stops it and passes it up to Kayden. He bolts to the Eagles' end. I go with Kayden.

An Eagles guy bumps Kayden from the side. He takes the puck back to our end. I'm like a dragon as I change direction and chase after him. My friend Nam and Emma are all over the Eagles players. Everyone is bunching up around our net.

Dad's voice is in my head–*stay open, buddy!*

I glide to the right side. The Eagles' number seven has the puck. He trips over his stick and crashes into Nam. The puck is loose. It's coming right at me!

This is it! My chance!

I rake the puck to me. Turn around. Skate to the Eagles' end. Everyone is crowded around our net still. I take the puck up the side.

It's just me. My heart is racing. I'm so fast. I'm a horse in the Vietnamese zodiac dashing across the ice.

I'm close to the net. Stop quick. Look at the far corner. Aim. And shoot!

The goalie dives toward me. The puck slides across the line.

I score!

I raise both hands in the air. My heart is bursting with joy, and everyone is cheering and clapping. It's my first goal of the season!

"Way to go, Jacob!" Kayden says behind me. I high-five him and Emma and Nam too.

My shift ends, and I skate back to the bench and look over at the bleachers. Grandpa Nội claps. He holds up four fingers on each hand. I know he means my jersey number. "Number eight lucky!" Grandpa Nội said when I first got it last month in October. Usually, only Dad comes to my games. I love when Grandpa Nội comes too.

After the game, I feel okay that we lost. I scored!

"You saw it? My goal?" I ask Dad as he helps me take off my hockey stuff in the dressing room.

"Great job, buddy. Up the side! Like I said!" He smiles.

Dad keeps saying he wanted to play hockey when he was a kid, but he was too poor. So he's really excited. He used to like hockey more than I did, but now I like hockey a lot.

Nam and his dad are beside us. "Good goal, Jacob!" Nam's dad, Chú Van, adds.

"Cám ơn, Chú." I say thank you, one of the only things I can say in Vietnamese.

As Dad takes off my helmet, my hair gets stuck.

"Ouch, Dad!" I rub my head.

Dad starts to take off my neck guard and shoulder pads. "Your hair. We have to cut it or tie it."

"I don't want to cut it. It's the helmet." I swing

my legs, pretending I'm a monkey playing around. "It's too small."

"I guess you'll need a new one. We'll go this weekend." He takes off my skates.

"I know what kind I want." I look over at Emma as her mom puts her awesome helmet in her hockey bag.

New helmet! New team! This hockey year is going to be great!

About the Author

©Kalla Photography

Linda Trinh is a Vietnamese Canadian author who writes stories for kids and grown-ups. The story of the Trung Sisters always made her feel proud. They were strong and brave females who were Vietnamese like her, so she felt she could be strong and brave in her life too. While she doesn't do Taekwondo, she likes to run to keep active and has even completed a half-marathon once. She's still working on improving her headstand pose in yoga though. She spends a lot of time staring out her window, daydreaming, and pacing around the house, writing in her head way before she types out anything. She lives with her husband and two kids in Winnipeg.

About the Illustrator

Clayton Nguyen is an artist working on animated tv shows and films to bring imaginary characters and worlds to life. In a complete coincidence, Clayton also started drawing at an early age and has two older sisters, just like Jacob. Being the youngest sibling, he is still sometimes treated like the baby of the family. Some of his earliest memories of becoming interested in art come from watching TV shows like *Art Attack* and anime with his sisters after school. Nowadays, when he isn't drawing, you'll often find him playing video games or getting bubble tea in Toronto.